SHINICHI SUZUKI:
HIS SPEECHES AND ESSAYS

Alfred Publishing Co., Inc.
16320 Roscoe Blvd., Suite 100
P.O. Box 10003
Van Nuys, CA 91410-0003

ISBN 0-87487-588-9

Table of Contents

DISCOVERY OF THE LAW OF ABILITY AND THE PRINCIPLE OF ABILITY DEVELOPMENT

—Proof that talent is not inborn—

by

Shinichi Suzuki

For many years, many people have cherished the common belief that talent is inborn and each person has his own inherited quality or nature, that everyone has his individual character and talent which are superior or inferior from his birth, and that this inherited talent cannot be developed further afterwards, if it is inferior from the start.

This belief has been advocated as a theory by many scholars, but I realized about forty years ago that it is totally wrong. Since then I have endeavored to prove that talent is no accident of birth and every child can be highly educated if he is given the proper training. I have demonstrated good examples of highly developed children in music. I also have been appealing for people in the world to understand my idea. It is very difficult, however, to change what has been believed for such a long time, but I have never been defeated by the difficulty, never given up my belief. I have proven the fact that talent is not inborn and I nurtured and developed many children whom I accepted as my students without any test for musical ability. I taught them to become splendid musicians. Meanwhile I finally found the law of ability after long research of the principle for developing talent.

I realized the following:

1. Talent is acquired through the powerful function of "life force" (or the life-giving force or energy).

2. Talent is developed as the matter of physiology or brain-physiology which functions in a living organism in order to sustain its life and keep it growing.

The law of ability might be summarized as the following:

"A living organism acquires talent responding to the environmental stimulation from the outside and adapting itself to all things surrounding it. Talent is the production of the life force; therefore, there is no talent without stimulation which comes from the outside."

A newborn baby's life force absorbs all the things around him, such as his mother's way of speech, her way of feeling and thinking and so forth. We should notice that a child acquires his talent parallel with his growth through his life force, being fed with nourishment. A living organism would have to die if it could not adapt itself to the environment. When we know that talent in order to survive in the environment, adapting himself to all kinds of environmental stimulation which comes from the outside.

Through my experiences I firmly believe that the law of ability is quite true. It is an obvious fact that a child's ability is developed in physiological or brain-physiological way, just as a baby's body grows physiologically through the activities of his powerful life.

If you move to Alaska with your newborn baby and raise him in the cold Alaskan environment, he will adapt himself to the stimulation there and will gradually come to the ability to endure the severe cold,. A physiological change will emerge on his skin over his whole body in order to survive in Alaska. Of course, one or two weeks stay in Alaska is not long enough to cause this change in the baby's body. He will never be able to gain the ability to bear the coldness in such a short period, though he might gain some knowledge about the Alaskan coldness.

A baby who hears his mother talking every day absorbs everything into his make-up and imitates his mother's voice, pronunciation, intonation and accent, adapting his vocal cords and muscles around the mouth and so forth to the outside stimulation. Finally he becomes able to speak quite the same way as his mother, just like a copy of the mother. It is impossible for me to pronounce English sounds beautifully, because I was raised hearing my mother tongue of Japanese, not English.

I often say, "A person is the product of his environment."

Even primitive men who lived in the Stone Age had the potential to develop to a high level, but their potential was not stimulated by the environment more than the Stone Age. Everyone in those days, therefore, had to grow as primitive men of the Stone Age. They could not develop their abilities more than those in the Stone Age. This example explains the law of ability eloquently.

If you put today's baby into the Stone Age and raised it there, it would become like other Stone Age men. On the other hand, if you put today's baby into the future world of five thousand years later and if he were educated by highly civilized people, he would certainly develop to the same highly advanced level at that area.

I discovered the fact that the activities of the great life force can be used to develop children's abilities to a miraculously high level under good fostering from the very day of their birth. I would like, therefore, to emphasize the importance of education from zero years old. We should esteem and value LIFE more, and we should notice that every child has the wonderful potential to be highly educated.

Early Education For Young Children

Now I have to talk about education for young children more concretely. First of all, I can tell you how to surely make any child completely tone deaf.A child who is raised by a tone-deaf mother or grandmother and grows hearing their out-of-tune lullabies every day will surely become tone deaf. The child's active life force accurately acquires the out-of-tuneness from his mother's out-of-tune songs, just as he gains the wonderful ability of speaking his mother tongue fluently. He can absorb even the delicate accent of the dialect in the area he lives in.

Consequently, you can nurture a normal baby to become a completely tone-deaf child through making him hear records with out-of-tune music every day- though I have no desire to try this experiment, of course.

I have the firm belief that there is no inherited talent for music; therefore, we could make a child become either an excellent musician or a tone-deaf person according to the law of ability and principle of the life force activity. It was some forty years ago when I realized the law and I accepted two young children as my first violin students for experiment. They were nurtured by listening to Kreisler and Thibaud on records at home everyday. One boy, who was four years old at that time, is now a professor at Curtis Music School in the United States; his name is Toshiya Eto. The other boy, Koji Toyota, who was three years old, is now concertmaster of the Berlin Radio Symphonic Orchestra. It might be said that Kreisler and Thibaud were really their teachers, and I myself was just an assistant of the two celebrated musicians. The two boys were the successful products of my experiment on the law of ability. I would like to emphasize again that the great power of life activity is the mighty gift given to human beings.

A child who has no opportunity to listen to any good music gains nothing. If he listens to out-of-tune music, he will grow to have out-of-tune abilities in music. If he is raised in an atmosphere with beautiful music, he will become a person of noble character, fine sensibility and excellent ability. I have been convinced of this through my experiences of some forty years.

Now I would like the teachers who are using the Suzuki Method to be aware of the following two points:

(1) What make children acquire their wonderful abilities?

(2) How can teachers and parents nurture their children to become fine persons with high abilities?

I have already tries to give an answer to the first question. So some answers to the second question will be given in the following paragraphs.

The Law of Ability

My research on the law of ability and the Suzuki Method was motivated by a fact that astonished me greatly one day some forty years ago. Children everywhere in the world were speaking in their own language with ease. They had gained such excellent abilities as to speak with utmost fluency. "What was this all about?" This must be the result, I thought, that their abilities had been developed from the day of their birth. Every child has a wonderful potential to be educated very highly. I wondered why their abilities were so splendidly developed only in their mother tongue. On the day when I notice this fact I started researching what kinds of conditions lie in the education in which those wonderful abilities of the mother tongue can be cultivated from the day of their birth. The method called "The Suzuki Method" is the fruit of my research and the discovery of the law of ability is also a harvest.

The following two points are the basis for acquirement through the Mother Tongue ability.

(1) Some abilities are developed through hearing.

(2) Some abilities are developed through speaking.

The same is seen in music education:

(1) Some abilities are developed by hearing good music.

(2) Some abilities are developed by playing music.

Abilities in music, therefore, will be developed splendidly if children listen to music and practice playing every day as enthusiastically as they practice their own language. Students who are hardly developed in music are the result of neglecting to listen to music.

If you gave lessons on speaking the mother tongue to your child and neglected to give him any lessons on listening, what would be the result? Up to now these same methods in teaching music have been used in general. Highly developed sensitivity in music can never be gained through this sort of method.

Every spring I have to listen to a great number of tapes sent from various levels of graduating students all over Japan. This year there are 7900 graduating students. Among them there are some excellent students who are five or six years old and yet can beautifully play all the movements of Bach's first concerto.

This year I listened to Bach's entire concerto recorded on tape by a four year old girl who played with a little violin (size 1/16th) very well. From birth she was raised to hear the violin played by her sister and brother.

Thus her desire to play the violin had been fully brewing before she picked up her tiny violin to start her learning. Then she showed wonderfully rapid progress and enthusiasm in learning violin, enjoying daily practice with her brother and sister, and growing to become able to play Bach's Concerto at such a young age. She won such a high ability in music through the same way as she acquired her speaking ability of her mother tongue with ease.

This is one of many good examples of children nurtured under almost the same conditions and processes as children follow unconsciously when they learn their mother tongue.

I have often asked mothers to make their children listen to records over and over again as their home work, but it seems fairly hard to put it into practice. Only a few mothers have accepted this advice. Recently, however, the number of parents who are able to understand the importance of my suggestions is increasing. As a result, some children are proving wonderfully that my suggestion is really right — through their rapid progress in learning.

The Building Block System

Now I would like to talk about how we can develop children's ability of performance. When we observe the process of language acquirement in the mother tongue very carefully, it is obvious that the ability of acquiring the mother tongue grows and is expanded effectively through the building block system.

A child learns his first word one day, and he repeats it over and over again until it becomes a part of him as an ability. The he learns another word. After he has mastered these two words, he adds a new word to the two he has learned perfectly. He practices these words many times every day, then he accepts the challenge of another new word to master and so forth. This is the way a child acquires his speaking ability. The way of developing abilities in general is quite the same as that of learning one's mother tongue.

One ability is created first, then a new ability is built on it, and then another new one is put on top of the other, and so on one after another.

One ability which is sufficiently developed breeds another greater ability, and so on, one ability after another. Thus abilities are greatly expanded and become more powerful and functional. Teachers and parents should be aware of this.

This building block system is used by all Suzuki teachers, and children's abilities are cultivated and expanded steadily through this method. Children who are trained in this way, therefore, can play any of the pieces they have already learned, without rehearsal, anytime, anywhere. The children's memories also, are wondrously expanded.

Suzuki students must learn to play music by heart, and it becomes a habit with them. The teachers, however, teach how to read music also when their students reach the appropriate level. Until then they make it a rule to play without music in class. This procedure produces wonderful memory ability. A student who is trained by this method from the first and is developed in his memory ability can learn a new piece very quickly. Moreover, when he is taught how to read music afterwards, he can learn the music by heart in a very short time, and he can play it excellently without looking at printed music.

Through my long experiences I have seen many examples of children at thirteen or fourteen years of age who have acquired such high abilities of performance and splendid music sensitivity that they can play the first movement of Sibelius' concerto by heart beautifully and without any mistakes, after only one week of practice at home with the printed music. I have learned, through these examples, how wonderful it is to make a habit of practice without reading music at the early stage.

The Accompaniment Tapes*

For learning musical beat and the correct musical tempo I made tapes with piano accompaniment for all the pieces of Suzuki School Vol. 1. When the teacher judges that a child has practiced one piece enough, he gives the accompaniment tape for the piece and says to the child, "At the next lesson, please let me hear you play the piece with the accompaniment tape." The child can proceed to the next piece if he or she can play well enough with the accompaniment. This method has had a marvelous effect on the students' sensitivity for musical tempo and beat. It also enhances children's enthusiasm for music.

Practice With Me*

Children's abilities are developed at home. So Suzuki teachers, in the classroom, teach children how to practice correctly at home. The teachers, therefore, have to study how to make the children's home practice joyful. for that purpose I made the tapes called "Practice With Me," and many students have used them effectively. I recorded my playing of each piece from the Suzuki School Books and my explanations on how to practice the piece at home joyously.

*Both the "Accompaniment Tapes" discussed here and the "Practice With Me" tapes are no longer available outside of Japan

At the top of the tape I talk to our young students, "Now let's practice together. I will repeat my performance as many times as you want to practice with me. When you become able to play this piece very well, please play again with the piano accompaniment." Each tape has the piano accompaniment part after my instruction. This series of the tapes for home practice is not only helpful to parents who are at a loss as to how they should help their children practice at home, but also it brings effective results to children's development. This is one of the important features of the Suzuki Method.

Lessons In The Classroom

The most important thing in infant education is to make children motivated to learn. A teacher should try to do his best to make his class joyous and pleasant. We never scold children nor find faults with them. Who scolds his baby when it makes a mistake in speaking its mother tongue because of poor ability in speaking? It is natural that a baby cannot speak very well. In learning music, the same principle applies. Young children who are still poor in their ability of speaking, of course, cannot play musical instruments very well. So the teacher should have the children practice a familiar piece with him over and over again, sometimes saying jokingly, "You are doing very well, except for some bad points."

Needless to say, the responsibility to correct these faults is on the side of parents at home, and teachers in the classroom. In our institute three or four students are scheduled for the same time in each lesson. The teacher instructs one student at a time directly, while the other students observe. They can learn from observing others' lessons. Sometimes they can have a chance to study with more advanced students. They are probably affected and encouraged by the advanced students' performances.

This method develops children's abilities and helps children enjoy their lessons. Each lesson is not long. We teach just one vital point at a time to the student, so that he can practice it over and over again at home. We teach one point at one lesson thoroughly. If we do this, his abilities can be developed very highly. On the other hand, if we give two or three learning points at a time, children will surely fail to grasp the points. I have learned this through my experiences. Children can be greatly influenced by each other, so they have a tendency to lose their eagerness for learning when they are kept in a one-to-one-style lesson between one teacher and one student.

Solo Concert Day

The last week of every other month is the week for solo concert. There is no ordinary class this week. On Monday all the students of the Monday classes and their parents get together in a classroom for the concert. One Tuesday all the students of Tuesday classes and their parents get together, and so on.

On that day each student demonstrates the results of his two-month-long home practice with the accompaniment tapes. This concert is a very good chance for the students to show their improvement in from of their classmates and to learn from their friends' performances. They enjoy these periodic concerts very much. Applause and praise given by their friends motivate them to practice more at home. I noticed, through my experiences, that this sort of activity is very helpful in developing enthusiasm for steady practice among young learners.

I recommend that you occasionally this sort of concert. A teacher might well choose some pieces for the concert a month or so ahead and make his students practice them. The children can master two or three pieces thoroughly for a month, if the pieces are not long.

Group Lessons

Once a month at least, all the children in the class are called together, and they joyfully play together the pieces they have learned up to now. Through the group lessons they can effectively study musical beat, correct posture, beautiful tone, poise, etc.

These occasions are extremely effective, especially for small children, because they can play and learn with advanced students. Anyway, children like to play in a group and they learn, unconsciously, poise, musical beat, and how to make beautiful tone from the more advanced and excellently developed children.

Every year in March we hold a grand concert at the annual convention of the Japanese Talent Education Movement. Three thousand children from all over Japan perform together with perfect harmony without rehearsing beforehand. It is possible because the children have been trained through their usual lessons under the instruction of their regular teachers in their home towns all over Japan.

Presenting Graduation Tapes

Students of our system in Japan go through five graduation steps, from elementary to advanced. each student submits his recorded tapes to me when applying for graduation from whatever level he is in. This system of assigning the graduation pieces has proved to be very effective in motivating students' learning, because children practice enthusiastically aiming at the next graduation level, and they do their best for it.

This year we numbered seven thousand nine hundred graduates in violin, piano, cello and flute. I listened to all these graduation tapes sent from the graduates all over Japan and carefully checked them all. Of course, it is the teacher in charge of the student who judges whether or not the student deserves to graduate from his level. I, as president of the Talent Education Institute, just authorize his graduation according to his teacher's recommendation. No student who submits the tape can fail to graduate. We make it a rule that graduation certificates are granted to all the students who submitted the tapes. Then the graduation concerts are held in many districts in Japan.

The purpose of this system is to stimulate students' learning motivation. I firmly believe this system is very effective for the purpose of motivation, so I hope eagerly that teachers instructing children through the Suzuki Method will use this system positively in many parts of the world.

Tonalization

The research and teaching of vocalization is the most important aspect of vocal music. It is said that the quality of teaching of vocalization shows the quality, whether superior or inferior, of the teacher.

Since I noticed this some time ago, I have been applying the idea to my violin teaching. now I usually spend the first half if my individual lesson period each time on teaching the very basic techniques on how to produce beautiful and noble tone on the instrument, just as vocal music teachers do on vocalization. After that I give my student his lesson on the piece of music he is studying.

In vocal music teaching Vocalization is a technical term producing a beautiful voice, and the teaching method for it is established. We had no equivalent term, nor method for beautiful sound production from an instrument. However, I proposed to teachers of the Suzuki Method in the States that we should establish such a teaching method to produce beautiful tone and we should give it an appropriate name. Then they molded the new term, Tonalization. Since then I have been fond of using "tonalization", and I am emphasizing how to practice and teach beautiful tone production.

I have offered to the teachers in Japan what I have researched and developed on this subject. Now they also are teaching tonalization to their students, using the Research tapes on which I recorded the new procedures for it. I believe that these tapes are quite useful for the teachers to use in their further study on this subject. I hope from the bottom of my heart that a finer method of teaching tonalization—one that will be the finest—will be established as soon a possible through exchanging better ideas about it between teachers in the world and through cooperative studies on this subject. As a matter of fact, I can tell you that the students learning from teachers who have profoundly researched tonalization are all gaining excellent performance ability. It is very important for teachers to develop their students' abilities by teaching them how to produce correct and beautiful tone on the strings from the beginning of their learning.

The Research Tapes For Teachers

For some time, we Suzuki teachers in Japan have had research tapes which involve newly devised teaching procedures, techniques, instructions of tonalization and studies made by myself and other teachers. Using these tapes, we are endeavoring to research better ways for teaching children more effectively. They are really helpful for that purpose. In this way teachers all over Japan can gain the latest information and teaching methods. They also can learn greatly from the results of research made one after another by other teachers.

I believe that this "research-tape-system" is functioning as one of the most productive tactics for promoting our movement. I have a sincere desire for teachers all over the world, using the Suzuki Method, to establish an organization for offering successful education to every child in many parts of the world. We should be able to expect great progress for our movement if we have such a powerful organization and can offer the research tapes to all members as well as to those in Japan.

The Suzuki Method is not a fixed method, but is continuously progressing day by day. It is seeking better and newer ways to develop children's abilities to a much higher level in a joyous natural atmosphere in the easiest way possible. Every child can be well educated. Every child has such wonderful potential and powerful "life force" in him. Now, teachers from all over the world, let us study together how to nurture our children correctly and how to develop their abilities to the most splendid level.

The Law of Ability and the "Mother Tongue Method" of Education
(1973)

It was forty years ago when this astonishing fact occurred to me. Children everywhere in the world were speaking in their own language; moreover, they did this fluently, which required a very high level of proficiency. "What was this all about?" I asked myself. People generally have believed that a child who makes poor grades in school was just born that way. "Brainless and dull witted" was the common and unthinking reproof. And yet these same children, unless born with brain damage, found no difficulty in speaking such a complicated language as Japanese fluently. If they really had been brainless they would not have had the ability to speak as they did. What did it signify? Why did it appear the the 'mother tongue' ability could be taught with the greatest of ease to every child (that is, the ability to speak, to make the necessary sounds in the correct context, and not the ability to handle to intricacies of grammar), and yet why did they not do well in various subjects at school, acquiring this learning just as they did their language? What is this ability? Can it be acquired, or is it inborn? To inquire further, what does inborn mean? Is it really true that talent for such things as music, literature, painting or any of the other arts is inborn? Like everyone else, I believed at that time, forty years ago, that if a child did badly at school, he was either lazy, dull-witted, or brainless. And I also believed that talent was inborn.

*   *   *

From that very day I started to study this problem and observe the practicability of the "Mother Tongue" method:

- The environmental conditions and their influence on the new-born baby as it accustoms itself to the sounds of the 'mother tongue'.

- Teaching the child by constant repetition to utter its first sound. Usually 'mama mama mama' and so on.

- Everyday attitude of the parents after the baby starts to talk.

- Natural progress through daily practice.

- The skillfulness with which the parents build up enthusiasm in the child, and the happiness the child finds in acquiring its newfound ability.

As a result I learned that the natural method of teaching a child its mother tongue is a marvelous educational process. It fills the child with enthusiasm. It is a natural process in which practice continues from morning till night. The child feels none of the anguish that so often accompanies learning by conventional methods which are applied to other forms of education. What child would refuse to learn its "mother tongue", that is, quit this means of communication, because they found the routine dull? Every child in such an environment grows steadily and without mishap toward an involvement in this delightful ability, and responds according to the stimuli supplies it by the parents.

With this method, what human abilities might be developed! Superior environment; skill to build up enthusiasm; joy in practice and more practice. Surely the "Mother Tongue" method is the most outstanding example of the development of human ability.

— Experimental Class at Regular School—

Some time later I tried to adapt this method to music education for young children. I accepted a number of children without first auditioning them, and began to teach them violin experimentally, convinced that every child would develop. The children did show great progress and enjoyed the process. What has happened to those children of forty years ago, and how active they are now in all parts of the world, will be reported in a later chapter. Anyhow, the "Mother Tongue" method was capable of being adapted to music education as well as other lines of learning, and I felt more and more confident that this concept would stand the test of time.

*　　*　　*

Twenty-five years ago, I very eagerly wanted to have a school experiment conducted, using my "Mother Tongue" method in their daily routine, and I asked Principal Kamijo of a primary school in

Matsumoto if he might try it out. He graciously acceded to my request and the experiment in education was launched.

The school had four groups in first grade, and one was chosen as the experimental group. I suggested that no one should be 'failed', no drop-outs allowed, and one of the teachers, a Mr. Tanaka, was put in charge and the experiment was underway.

There was one child who could not even count up to three; she seemed to be somewhat retarded, but I did observe that she was speaking her native tongue with ease. I asked Mr. Tanaka not to fail her and I explained my method to him. He understood very well and saw this child through her difficulties so that by the time she reached fourth grade she was no different from any of the other children in a class of forty. Later she passed her entrance examination for high school, which presents no small challenge in Japan, where high school entrance examinations are highly competitive. This experiment, carried out in a regular primary school in Matsumoto, by regular teachers, certainly proved that it is possible to educate in primary school in such a way that no child need be dropped from a class.

It was clear that each child could develop his own abilities very successfully by the use of this method. In this class the following things were observed: No homework was assigned; the knowledge was absorbed to the degree that it became an unconscious effort, (each child 'made it his own' so to speak); the lessons were performed in an enjoyable atmosphere, and, most important of all, no child was ever made to feel inferior.

Unfortunately this class had to be abandoned after some four years, for Principal Kamijo died, and his successor had no belief in, or sympathy with the experiment, despite the urgent please of the parents and the children alike. the group was broken up and spread among the other classes, reverting to what was, in the eyes of the new principal, I have no doubt, a more conventional approach to education.

— Talent Education at Yoji Gakuen—

Next I would like to report on the experimental pre-school (that is, pre-primary school) methods we conduct at Talent Education Institute for the purpose of applying educational methods that develop children's individual abilities so that the ability becomes an integral part of the child. Twenty-five years ago I founded in Matsumoto the Talent Education Institute for pre-school children, called in Japanese 'Yoji Gakuen', and invited Mrs. Yano, an educator in this part of the country, to start the project in this method of learning so that every child might develop his ability to the point where it becomes a part of him. The children were, and are, accepted without any tests. This school has been continuing for twenty-five years. There are sixty children in the class, comprising in age those of three, four and five years. we do no separate them according to age, which normally is done in regular schools, because we know very well that the three year olds grow up steadily under the stimulating environment afforded by the older children. In one year, they usually acquire the ability to memorize one hundred and seventy to one hundred and eighty haiku, and they are able to repeat any one of them clearly upon demand. A haiku is a short Japanese poem of five, seven and five syllable in three lines. Of course, we train them to develop many other abilities, such as physical education and the development of quick reflexes, writing numbers correctly, and reading kanji. Drawing and calligraphy are taught as is English conversation. They are also taught to speak their mother tongue, Japanese, clearly and correctly. To do this we use the same training methods as are used to train T.V. announcers. To observe the enthusiasm and happiness of these tiny children is the deepest source of satisfaction for those who work with them. during the last seven years we have tested the I.Q. (Tanaka-Binet system) for the five year olds who graduate from pre-school to primary first grade. The average I. Q. has been near 160. In 1973 the average was 158.

The many parents who have heard about this school are flocking to enter their children until, at this moment, we are fully loaded for the next four years. The children who will be enrolled four years from now are as yet unborn.

To sum up: The "Mother Tongue" method leads the child, by repeated stimulation, to develop an ability and make it his own. If a young child is taken to Alaska where he is raised in the cold climate, the stimulation of the cold environment over a period of years will develop his ability to endure on his skin and over his whole body the frigid temperature. On the other hand, if the child's experience of the cold weather in Alaska is brief, then the child, on returning to Tokyo, will have only learned about a cold experience and will have not been able to make the ability to endure cold as a part of his own makeup. The child, educated to use this method of learning, will find that it can be brought into play in building other abilities as well. It is somewhat similar to the theory of principal and interest. Interest produces more money and more money produces more interest which, in turn, produces still more interest.

Now comes the physical side of it all. In the example of the child and his experience in Alaska, it is realized that this experience of building the ability to withstand the cold actually was a physiological one. I would like to think that the "Mother Tongue" method can also be regarded as physiological, the only difference in the experience being the difference between air and sound, on the one hand developing, through constant experience the ability to endure cold and, on the other, through constant experience of sound the ability to speak one's mother tongue. It seems to me that the interaction between parent and baby, the sharing of their lives, the parent's mind, senses, and the functions which the baby instinctively learns and makes its own, are also entirely physiological. I do not know whether this subject is in the field of physiology of the brain or not, but from my experience I am disposed to think so.

— Why So Many Dropouts?—

The method and the aim of education must become different from that which the child regularly experiences in primary school today. And it cannot be repeated too often that the several abilities of the children must be developed to the degree that they form a part of their makeup. what is happening in primary schools is that set curriculum is adhered to at any cost without regard to the human equation.

Increasingly difficult material is forced on the children as a routine matter, and some children, unable to keep up the pace, become deeply discouraged, give the impression of being retarded, and eventually drop out. And too often, the parent, not being in the close relationship with the child which we stress at Talent Education Institute, is apt to dismiss this distressing situation, saying "Well, he was born that way and I can't help it." Unfortunately this attitude is all to prevalent throughout the world, and it accounts, I am sure, for the number of underdeveloped children we encounter.

This underdevelopment is due to the failure of education at home, starting from the baby's first cry. If young plants are damaged, we know quite well what the result will be. If we damage young lives we should also know what the result will be. I look for the day when nations will give much more attention to this most important subject, so important to national well-being, and implement a national policy that ensures proper development. As I have pointed out in this section dealing with the serious matter of 'drop-outs', the differing abilities of first graders is a very serious matter.

Under our present system the children, varied in abilities, including the capacity for learning, are thrown together in one class and, as pointed out before, advanced without regard to their capacity for developing an ability and making it a part of themselves. This method produces many difficulties and frustrations for the teachers also. They sense that what is taking place is bound to produce a lack of enthusiasm in the child, a feeling of disappointment leading to complete indifference and, eventually, to dropping out. In our talent Education Institute we teachers have a warning phrase, "To force and 'manuals' (the curriculum) is to produce the 'drop-out'." In Japanese the word for 'education' is kyoiku. Kyo means to teach, and iku means to bring up. There is considerable subtlety here when we become aware that "teaching" produces drop-outs and "bringing up" produces well balanced children, and that the two combine to make a child's ability his very own. We must realize that "Mother Tongue" method is what this is all about.

*   *   *

Let us return to Mr. Tanaka and his first grade at the primary school mentioned before in the experimental class, which was guaranteed not to produce or allow drop-outs. The initial lessons of the first graders were recognized as of vast importance. Just as in the beginning of learning the mother tongue, the start was kept very slow. Extremely easy material was chosen at the start, and all the children accomplished what was set with no mistakes and full marks. This was a start in building confidence and enthusiasm. He make sure that every child understood the material and made no mistakes.

He stressed, trained and practiced this theory of 'no mistakes'.

Further he realized, as we all know, that small children have a short attention span. Some children became bored or inattentive after five or six minutes. When this happened, say, in the math lesson he would immediately switch to language, and when the attention of a child appeared on the wane in this subject, still another was chosen. At the end or a year these young children had developed the ability to concentrate on any one subject for some forty-five minutes!

In language he would repeat the training five times a day for periods of five to ten minutes. He would first give them eight words to learn (with no mistakes), and when each child had learned them and made them his own, he would add two more. Thus they would practice the original eight along with two new ones. Additions were made in such fashion during the learning of their first book. When I was informed that this was accomplished, I went to the school to observe the class at work. The children sat with their books in front of them, but closed. Mr. Tanaka called on a child to read Lesson 12.

The child stood up and recited clearly and correctly without any mistakes and without recourse to the book. Then another one did the same with the Lesson 17. During the time they had been engaged with learning their first book they had, of course, learned not only to read but to write. So he directed the whole class to write Lesson 18, which they did easily and well, and at a remarkably fast tempo. If this method, with which I had asked Mr. Tanaka to experiment, is used, every child will grow, full of enthusiasm, encouraged and fired with the joy of study, which will grow like a snowball of discovered abilities. I used exactly the same method in the teaching of music, producing no drop-outs. Every child can be developed.

A Report on My Experiment

I started to study the "Mother Tongue" method and began applying it to teaching the violin some forty years ago, convincing that every child could be developed if taught this way.

I accepted children without first auditioning them and trained them along the lines of the "Mother Tongue" method or, as it is called in Western Countries, the "Suzuki Method". The first pupil I worked with was the four year old Toshiya Eto.

Next was the three year old Koji Yoyoda followed by the Kobayashi brothers, Hidetaro Suzuki, Takaya Urakawa, and many others, all accompanied by their enthusiastic and co-operative parents. They all made rewarding progress. At eleven years of age, Toshiya Eto won the prestigious Mainichi Shimbun award.

I have never pressed any of my young charges to enter the professional field. This is not my aim in education, but, at the same time, I have never deterred those who felt the urge, and many of the original students went abroad to study professionally with distinguished teachers in the United States, France, Belgium and Germany. They have gained high positions in the realm of string instruments. Toshiya Eto is known throughout the world as an outstanding soloist. Koji Toyoda is now concertmaster of the Berlin Radio Symphony orchestra.

Takeshi Kobayashi is concertmaster of the Czechoslovakian Symphony; Kenji Kobayashi concertmaster of the Oklahoma Symphony, Urakawa of the Bamberg Symphony. There was a time when the Japanese people were assumed by Westerners to be most unmusical, and indeed, from the Western point of view this was once true.

Never having been exposed to Western music they knew nothing of it. However, no one had looked into the fact that the average Japanese child is able to speak this mother tongue long before he can read it. As I have explained at length, this was the truth which gave me the clue to the so-called "Mother Tongue" method of education, not just in music education, but in all branches of training. My story of the preliminary experiment in the primary school in Matsumoto makes this clear. Applying the "Mother Tongue" method to musical education of the aforementioned group, among the first to be so exposed, I found further evidence of the effectiveness of the method. Realizing that every child born into this world has ability of one sort of another (that is, of course, with the exception of those tragically retarded) and that the "Mother Tongue" method can be used in their education, I have often pondered whether or not if all nations and races were to concern themselves more with this type of education, a much better atmosphere of understanding and peace among men might be the end product.

We all know how strongly my very close friend, the late Pablo Casals, believed in this ideal of brotherhood and the great part that music could play in it.

The Law of Ability

In conducting observations, I have thought about what the source of ability might be, and have come to the conclusion that it is the great power of life itself. This great power of life governs physical growth. It imparts ability during the growth process, which responds to outside stimulation so that life can be sustained. This stimulation enables the child to develop his ability as a part of his make-up. This great power of life governs every function of the body, which is centered in the brain, an organ with capabilities far beyond any computer. I can no longer bring myself to believe in what is commonly referred to as an inborn talent, be it musical, literary or any other form. My forty years of experiments in child education have persuaded me against such a belief.

I have no doubt that people are born with hereditary physiological differences, but I believe that a person's abilities grow and develop depending on stimulation from the outside. Babies, whether born in primitive times or in contemporary times, start at the same point and receive environmental stimulation according to their respective periods, growing up as adults suited to the era in which they live.

It would be true therefore, to say that a baby born in the twentieth century, but nurtured and raised by stone age people in a stone age environment, would develop abilities that would correspond with that age. I am often asked what I consider to be the limits of growth in a child's ability. I do not know what the limits are, but I am persuaded that the child's ability can grow to the level mankind can reach, by the time man's history terminates. As a practical answer, I would say that a child can, at the very least, develop all his various abilities to the high level of his ability in using his mother tongue. And this level is very high.

*   *   *

I have learned that musical ability is not inborn, and that it is possible to raise a child to be tone deaf or to raise the child to have superior musical ability. Imagine, if you will, a Mozart or a Beethoven brought up from birth with cacophony, to every variety of unmusical sound. My own observations tell me that we would not have had a Ninth or a Jupiter Symphony. Thus any child similarly exposed would grow up tone deaf. Children raised in Osaka, hearing their parents talking every day, grow up with all the delicate differences of the Osaka dialect, and those in Tokyo acquire a Tokyo dialect. There are only human beings in the human family, and the word 'genius' is a term of respect we apply to those who have made an outstanding success of the abilities that they have acquired as they grew up under good fostering.

Some claim that, as a result of heredity, a person has it in him to be a musician, an artist, a writer; that the talent is inborn and, in some cases, amounts to a 'natural genius'. I just do not believe this. When one considers all the babies that are given the miracle of life and the power to live, it is saddening to see those who are improperly brought up, where their kind of education has failed them from the age of zero years old, without beneficial environmental stimulation, and who are judged by unthinking people to have been born that way.

31

It is an ancient Japanese custom to catch a wild baby nightingale in the mountains and place it in association with a domesticated bird, one with a particularly beautiful song. The wild creature from the mountains hears this excellent singing every day and in due time it, too, is giving forth the sounds it has been listening to. On the other hand, if the bird has for too long heard the croaking of the mother bird, then the capture of the little creature will prove to be too late, and the subsequent attempt to train it as described above will end in failure. This is another example of the Law of Ability.

In Japan there are thousands of babies who listen daily to a recording of the first movement of the Mozart Serenade for string orchestra. The parents report to me that it is not very long before a very strong and deeply pleasurable reaction is observed, and by the time the child is some for or five years old, it is responding to the music with joyous movement. In the same way, and at the same time, the baby is absorbing every emotion the parents display to it: 'The fate of the children is in the parents hands.' It is at once a wonderful and critical responsibility, since children absorb into their make-up everything from their environment.

*   *   *

Some children are brought up by parents who seem to believe the the proper way to raise them is by a regime of persistent scolding and bullying. In accordance with the Law of Ability, the children develop their own ability to be scolded and therefore, develop resistance. It is a frightening thing, and the eventual outcome causes the parents to wonder why their child was born so obstinate. Of course the child was not born so. It has developed its own ability to be obstinate.

An Appeal of a World Policy of Child Development

In October of 1968 at the Assembly hall of the United Nations in New York I appealed to those gathered there to consider the necessity of a worldwide policy of proper child development, education and care. I explained the every child is influenced from the moment of birth by its own environment and that every child can be developed. But there is only one way.

In every country in the world today there are countless parents who, in ignorance of proper child training, are raised miserable, twisted personalities. It is one of the most urgent problems of our time, and appears to be mankind's major blind spot. When one considers the important part for good or evil that this future citizen of the world will play, I am unable to understand who the nations forsake such a critical task.

I wish countries of the entire world could establish and carry out national policies for child training and care as quickly as possible. When you contemplate a carefully cultivated green field and think of the care taken in the raising and cultivation of it, you cannot help but wonder that all that went into that project should be denied to children; whereas if they, too, received the care that the field had received, they would grow up to be good human beings with their respective abilities highly developed, who would build a good society.

But the raising and educating of children must be founded on a proper knowledge of how all this is to be accomplished. If the situation is left as it is now, and we fail to raise the 'young plants' as they should be raised, then I do not see how one can expect to have good nations in this world. Without good people you cannot have good nations. As a national policy it is the first imperative that instructors should be stationed throughout the country in the cities, towns and villages, and that as soon as a new baby is registered at the appropriate offices, the instructor should visit the family and teach the parents the best way to bring up the child both in matters in health and in the developing of its abilities from the very beginning. The parents should be taught how to do all this on their own and have a deep personal involvement with the child. The instructor his territory regularly, give further guidance and assistance to the parents, and watch the child's development. If such a system were to be established, and if the children of the world were accorded such care, guidance, parental relationship and sense of responsibility, then, I am convinced, the world would start to change greatly. I ended by urging my listeners to give this very important matter their earnest consideration for the sake of children all over the world. I was accorded a warmhearted ovation, but I could not help wondering which country would be the first to take a step in this direction. I wish it were possible to believe it might happen at least by the twenty-first century!

Some four years ago I, along with Mr. Masaru Ibuka, Chairman of Sony Corporation and a strong believer, visited the then Prime Minister Sato at his official residence and discussed with him for about an hour the need for a national policy of child development. Although he displayed considerable interest, it is sad to relate that nothing came of it. If such a national policy could be carried out in as many countries as possible (and, of course, I would like to see Japan in the lead) I think that in twenty to thirty years a great change in the world would be seen. The love that parents have for their children would be awakened to proper child development through the guidance of trained instructors, and good character and ability would be promoted in every home. By these means I am certain that many children on this earth would be saved. When it is realized that babies can be raised in many different ways, it is clear that the manner of bringing up children is the responsibility of all adults in the world.

I would like to ask that scholars and educators clarify the concept that ability is not inborn, and dismiss the common error of assuming that failure in a child is due to its being born that way. Failure is not inborn and ability is not inborn. There is the story of the two little savage girls, three and four years of age who were raised in the wilds by wolves and, of course, behaved like wolves. There was nothing inborn there; they absorbed the outside stimulation, developed a wolf-like ability and made it their own!

One more request I would make is that educators study the "Mother Tongue" method and develop ways for the abilities of children to grow in the same manner as all children acquire the complex ability to speak their mother tongue, thereby ushering in as early as possible the age when the tragedy of the 'drop out' will have been abolished from our system of education.

I have already spent forty years exerting efforts in this direction, but as a layman, I can do very little. Scholars and professional educators with their great influence, can exercise great leadership in changing the world.

Speech given to the
Music Educators National Conference
March 1964
Philadelphia, Pennsylvania

Outline of
Talent Education Method

by Shinichi Suzuki
President of the Talent Education
- Institute in Japan

Most people seem to think, even now, that one may not become a successful musician unless he has musical talents. That is to say, they think all successful musicians have been born with musical talents. I cannot agree with this. This idea of mine started 27 or 28 years ago, and it was at that time that I started on Talent Education.

Mr. Toshiyo Eto, who is now teaching at the Curtis Academy of Music in Philadelphia, was my first child-pupil. His father brought him to me when Toshiyo was only 4 years old. It was my first experience in teaching such a young pupil and I was quite concerned about it. The thought that came to my mind at that time as in regard to a child's mother tongue. A child will learn to speak Japanese when he is born and reared in Japan. The normal child can use more than 3,000 words at the age of six. This would certainly indicate that the brain of a normal child is quite active. This the the same the world over. I thought at that time that this fact should be of great importance to mankind. We should always keep in mind that few children are born mentally deficient.

Now let us turn to the talent of a child. Do Japanese babies have an aptitude for Japanese as soon as they are born? No. If a Japanese baby is born in England or America and brought up by English-speaking parents, that baby is the case with any baby, regardless of national origin. That is to say—any child will learn any language according to the conditions in which that child is reared. Every child has the capacity to be taught. This is how it learns its mother tongue.

I have studied very closely how a baby learns to speak, and have tried to work out some method according to these basic rules. I call this "the educational method of the mother tongue" and I have used this method for teaching music.

Toshiyo Eto was the first pupil who was taught according to this method. Musical talent is something that comes after birth. In order to prove this, let me speak about my experience.

I let a newborn baby listen to classical music. For example, a Brandenburg concerto or a Tchaikovsky serenade or a Beethoven quartet. I choose one movement from such classics and let the baby listen to the same tune every day. In about five months time the baby will memorize this melody. If you do not believe this, try it yourself.

It is very easy to test whether the infant has memorized the melody or not. To relate one of my experiences: A certain friend of ours had a baby. At that time its sister was six years old and she would practice the first movement of Vivaldi's G minor concerto every day. I visited their home when the baby was five months old. The baby was in a good mood in the mother's arms. So I decided on the test. I played Bach's *Minuetto*. The baby looked happy. In between I switched to the first movement of Vivaldi, which the baby was always hearing. At the first three notes, the baby moved his whole body in time with the music and looked much happier. He clearly distinguished these two melodies.

We should try to let babies listen to good music and to nurture a good music sense as early as possible.

Let me here explain how a nightingale is trained to sing well. If we catch a very young, wild nightingale in the Spring and put a good-voiced nightingale beside it for about 30 days, the throat of the baby nightingale changes so that it will be able to sing like its teacher. By changing the surroundings, the wild bird will change in order to fit the new situation. If we use a gramaphone to train a nightingale, the bird will sing accordingly—even imitating the sound of the needle going over the surface of the record.

Almost the same may be said of human beings. Children listen to the pronouncing of words by their parents and their vocal chords adjust themselves physiologically to make the same kind of pronunciation as their parents. The pronunciation of English by a Japanese child and an American child is different. This is because the physical adjustment has not been made by the Japanese child.

To give a bad example: If a nightingale that sings poorly is kept close to a young nightingale for some time, the young bird will learn to sing poorly. This is one basic rule.

From my tests of twenty years, I have found that young children who have been given a chance to listen to good music acquire a good sense of music—just like naturally being accustomed to their mother tongue. We should realize that even a child of six has been receiving for six years. From a musical point of view, the child can be educated by good music, bad music, or no music at all.

When we teach the violin to a six-year-old child, we have to admit there is a difference in musical abilities. There are children who learn quickly and children who are rather slow. Most people seem to think that the difference if because of the musical talent (or inheritance) of the child, but I do not wholly agree with this. I think that we should remember that the child is getting education from the time it it is born. In Talent Education, we warn all parents that education can not be started too soon. Our motto is: the sooner, the better.

Another basic rule is: If we do not educate at all, the child will learn nothing. For instance, the talent for music can only be had by cultivating it and can not be achieved by itself. This is my conviction.

If music talent could be acquired naturally, the cultural history of mankind would have been quite different, I am sure. Children born in the Stone Age were educated under a low degree of culture. Children educated by a high degree of culture grow up to have all sorts of talents. The level of the children of the Stone Age and of today is different. Children re-act according to education and it is up to us to find the best method of education.

The seed for music should be sown early by this new method. Talent Education, so that it will turn out to be a talent after the child has grown up.

Let us think of how talent is cultivated. I like to use the phrase "capacity of the brain" to mean the capacity to achieve talent and to use it. To discover the "capacity of the brain" is one point we have yet to solve in all the problems we have in regard to education. Scholars of heredity may say that the talents for music, mathematics or literature are there when the baby is born, but I wish to disagree on this point. My reason is that the matter of heredity is within the limit of psychological conditions, whereas culture, built up by mankind, cannot be passed on, physically.

I wish to define the meaning of the phrase "brain capacity" to mean the ability to catch one's surroundings and to realize it. In other words, to take in things outside of oneself and to work it into a sort of energy within one's self and bring it out by actions. In this sense, what I wish to call superior heredity will mean more speed and delicacy in catching things outside oneself. Brains that have no speed or are dull are what I consider inferior heredity. I wish to divide the classification of heredity by the above standard. That, I believe, is the reason why the result is not the same even when the children are educated under the same conditions.

This is to say that a child with good heredity will not grow up to be a highly educated man if his education is only on the same level with that of the Stone Age. If is only with high educational levels that well-educated man can be made. History tells us that this is true and I believe the same way be said for the future. Because we do not know the future standard of civilization, we cannot estimate how high an education the new born child will be able to receive and achieve. The capacity and possibilities are so great. I like to call this "the unlimited height."

All parents interested in Talent Education should look upon their children with this thought always in mind. So, in educating their children, in whatever field it may be, the most important point is that the parents should realize that the child has unlimited possibilities according to the education that is given the child. This is what I wish to tell all parents: If your child has already started to speak, please believe in the bright brains and abilities of your child.

We must always be thinking of new and better methods in order to give a better and higher education to our children.

In cultivation, the most important thing is the seedling. The whole future of the plant depends mostly on the seedling—how big the tree will grow, how much fruit it will bear, etc.

Although this is a fact known by everyone, so few parents think in this way when the matter concerns their own children. It seems a pity that we do not realize and utilize this knowledge in regard to the education of our own children.

It is often said that children who are bad in arithmetic are stupid, dull. This is jumping to the wrong conclusion. Why do we not teach arithmetic by the same method that we teach our mother tongue? A child will learn four or five words and use them quite freely. Ability to use the words comes only from using them. A few words can be increased gradually and naturally. Then ten words will become the basis for the next increase. This is the method by which the mother tongue is learned by the child.

I have tried out my new method of teaching arithmetic at some primary schools. We taught about 40 pupils by what I call "The full-mark method." We teach until every pupil in the class gets full-marks (100%) and education begins from this stage. We teach how easy it is to get full-marks and the method we use is the same as teaching the mother tongue. According to our tests of teaching arithmetic for five years, we found that all pupils were able to get full marks, every time without exception.

This is the method I use to teach music. I think that success in education can be attained when all parents believe in the capacity of their children at a very early stage, and start education as soon as the baby is born. It will be a success when our society becomes this way.

The final objective of Talent Education is to cultivate artistic appreciation in a child, not to make a musician out of every child we teach. It is a movement started by myself and carried on by parents who want to bring up their children to have a refined human character. Please be eager and serious in the education of your child and give full cooperation to your child's teacher—this is my message to parents.

"Any Child Can Be Tone Deaf"

from

Children and Talent (circa 1965)

Any human being in the world will grow up to be tone-deaf if he is brought up from the day of his birth for twelve or thirteen years hearing every day only records of music played out of tune. This is for exactly the same reason that children in Osaka, who every day hear nothing but the Osaka dialect as they grow up, with all without exception speak the Osaka dialect as adults. For this same reason also, the children brought up in different regions all around the world all grow up to be expert connoisseurs of the delicate pronunciations and melodies of the speed native to the region of the country in which they were raised.

If a newly born baby is played a record of a Vivaldi violin concerto every day whenever it cries, the baby will have learned the concerto well after four or five months. The same thing is true if the baby is brought up listening to a Bach concerto.

This method of training is being put into practice today everywhere in Japan.

This fact entirely demolishes the common-sense notions that we have long held about the inborn talents of human beings, since it proves that there is no such thing as a person literally born with a special aptitude, such as an inborn talent for music.

This is because a person either becomes tone-deaf, or grows to have a superior appreciation of music, depending on the method in which he was trained, that is, depending on his environment. Therefore, we are left with the simple fact that abilities are gradually acquired through the operation of the adaptive powers which enable human beings to adjust to their environment.

The facts adduced above prove that this is not a question of musical talent alone, but rather that talents in general are acquired, not inborn.

Thus, the human mind, literary talent, mathematical talent, and other talents as well, are all developed according to post-natal conditions.

Life Activities Develop Abilities

Man is endowed with life amid natural surroundings, and lives his life adapting himself to his natural environment as well as to the cultural environment created by man himself. Thus, I believe that culture is merely a part of man's environment and nothing more.

Living beings must adapt themselves to their environments in order to live; the efforts at adaptation are constantly accompanied by changes from moment to moment, and life is preserved while constant physiological adaptations are being performed. Therefore, in the long run, I believe that environmental changes also occasion hereditary changes by means of human physiological adaptations, thus actually creating the history of human life.

With regard to the idea that culture is merely a part of environment, I might add that a baby who is raised in an extremely low temperature and exposed to cold winds grows up to be an adult able to withstand the cold very well. I think that the same conditions apply to a person who is constantly exposed to the special air currents called music and who grows up to be a person with the ability to withstand music.

To sum up, we could express in simple terms what we have said above about the prime forces causing abilities to develop and the conditions for their development in the following manner:

1. What develops abilities? Life activities.

2. How? By adapting to the environment in order to live.

3. Why are there superior and inferior abilities?
Because of inferior or superior life activities
(through heredity).

Thus, in my opinion, the conditions mentioned above decide the way in which various superior or inferior abilities are developed in individuals out of their respective environments.

For this reason, if a person with highly superior life activities is born in the Stone Age and brought up in a Stone Age environment, he will, despite his superior potentialities, grow up into a person with abilities appropriate to the Stone Age. Even a person with far inferior life activities to the Stone Age man will grow up to be a person with incomparably higher cultural abilities if he is raised in the environment of the society of today. On the other hand, if a contemporary baby, born in our day, were to be raised in an environment of Stone Age people, he would be entirely unable to display the cultural traits of today, but would grow up instead to be a person with entirely Stone Age abilities and sensitivities.

All Children Are Wonderful

All children everywhere in the world are born with wonderful life activities.

These wonderful innate abilities develop according to the training given them. They grow rapidly day by day, hour by hour, in conformity with the environment.

One day, about 30 years ago, the following fact was brought (home) to my mind with a terrific impact:

"All children possess the potentiality of being trained to superior abilities."

And it is a fact that Talent Education in language has been given to growing children in every corner of the globe for thousands of years. All children are educated superbly in this way.

This fact reveals the following truth:

"If only they are trained skillfully, in the same way as they are educated in their own native language, all children throughout the world can develop their native abilities."

Until that day, I had been asleep in the common-sense notions handed down to me. But on that day 30 years ago, I was not only startled, but I also awoke.

Do Not Spoil the Seedlings

Many parents who do not know how vast are the human being's potentialities and how to develop these potentialities properly are unconsciously neglecting to foster their children's growth at the proper time, and are thus ruining their children. All growth begins from the very day of birth.

If the seedling is spoiled, nothing can be done about the sad fate of that plant or being.

Abilities develop only for things which have been experienced. But we must not forget how a seedling grows, about it fate, and about how it can be spoiled.

When we view growth from the standpoint of education, while we sense the wonder and the promise of something growing, we are at the same time struck by the fearsome idea that the momentary changes undergone by a human being in his formative period are irrevocable.

We cannot help being deeply impressed by the profound importance of educational methods for children in their early period of growth and formation.

When the facts were published at Yale University in 1940 about Kamala, the little girl who was raised in the mountains of India by wolves until she was seven years old, they must have given much food for reflection to all parents of children. Kamala, who had been raised in conformity to the life environment of wolves, had grown up into a human being with a wolf's senses, a wolf's abilities. After her seventh year she was raised by Rev. Singh, but in a period of four whole years she was able to learn only six words.

After the past has once been formed, nothing can be done to change it......

One wishes to ask those parents who are resigned to the fact that their children are "not intelligent," what kind of superior conditions they have provided for their children, or whether, after all, they have neglected them and refused them opportunities.

If a child's abilities have developed well enough for him to learn to speak Japanese, then how can he possibly be an inborn ignoramus? Inferior abilities occur when children like Kamala pass their formative period in an environment in which their abilities, except for language abilities, atrophy because of lack of experience. Their sad fate has already begun at this early stage.

Conclusion

Let us begin to educate all children from the very day they are born. The fate of a child is in the hands of his parents. Every child has been born with high potentialities.

The greatest duty, and the greatest joy given to us adults is the privilege of developing these potentialities and of educating desirable human beings with beautiful, harmonious minds and high sensitivity.

There is always a bright tomorrow waiting in the future for humanity. Someday, without fail, the day will come when all children in the world will be educated and trained to be happy human beings. I have not the slightest doubt that someday human society will be organized so that each person will consider it his greatest joy in life to live for the happiness of others.

When I think of man's essential readiness to develop into any type of person in accordance with his environment, then I am strongly impressed with the great love and blessings showered by Nature upon mankind.